COAL FOR
KIERA

AWARD WINNING AUTHOR
E.M. SHUE

COAL FOR KIERA

E.M SHUE

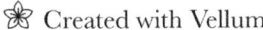 Created with Vellum

INTRODUCTION

Welcome to Santa Claus, Indiana where Christmas isn't just a holiday, it's a way of life. Join these 12 amazing authors with 11 wonderful books as they bring you some instalove, a little mystery, and maybe some thriller, for a romance filled holiday!

The community of Santa Claus was designed in 1849. The story of how it received the name of Santa Claus has roots both in fact and legend. In January 1856 the town applied for a post office to be installed.

On June 25, 1895, as part of a nationwide standardization for place names, the post office name was changed to the one word *Santaclaus*. The town's unique name went largely unnoticed until the late 1920s, when Postmaster James Martin began promoting the Santa Claus postmark. The name was changed back to *Santa Claus* on February 17, 1928. It was then that the Post Office Department decided there would never be another Santa Claus Post Office in the United States, due to the influx of holiday mail. The growing volume of holiday mail became so substantial that it caught the attention of Robert Ripley in 1929, who featured the town's post office in his nationally syndicated *Ripley's Believe It or Not!* cartoon strip.

Learn more about this unique town here: https://santaclausind.org

To all those that struggle during the holidays.
This is for you.

CHAPTER 1
KIERA

The rain feels like it's seeping into my skin through my coat
and clothes. I shiver and look around the dark country road. I
have music playing in one ear while the other listens for an
approaching car. There are no lights this far from town. In the
distance, I can just make out the shape of our old mailbox; it's
rusting and falling apart. My father, Leon, won't replace it, and
I can't find it in my heart to care.

I stop to check for mail when I reach the end of our driveway.
Leon has been marking my mail "Return to sender" lately.
The man will do anything to screw with me. I slide my gloved
hand across the bottom surface and out slides an envelope. In
the faint moonlight, I can make out the words "Not at this
address" scrawled above my name. I look at the return address
and cringe; I'm so glad I caught this before it got sent back. It's
from an apartment management company in Chicago. I had
emailed them my application a couple weeks

ago. I can't wait to see what they said. With my heart lifted, I make my way down the dark gravel drive, careful of the many potholes filled with rainwater. A light flashes in the darkness, and I trip and stumble into a puddle. My sneakers are now both soaked and I have to work early in the morning. Shit! I look up to see light flash across the darkness again. It's coming from the television in the living room. Leon is waiting up for me.

I step off the driveway into the brush, hoping I can hide. I've tried to avoid him in the four days since my eighteenth birthday when he threw me out of the house, as if I had a place to go. Leon has been drunk and belligerent in that time. Every day from the time I was twelve, he's made sure I know how much he hates me. He didn't always hate me, though. My father loved me at one time. In fact, he thought I was the most perfect baby...until I turned a week old and my momma died. Then everything changed. Momma's sister took me in and raised me. I only had to see Leon once a month when my aunt would make us have dinner together. I never got to know my mom, but I've been told by many people, including my aunt, that she was as artistic as I am.

My dream is to own my own studio someday. I'll sell other artists' paintings, as well as my own.

According to my aunt, my mom painted many paintings, but I've only seen some of them...once. I had needed something of hers for a school project when I was fourteen. Leon had told me I couldn't have anything, that I didn't deserve any of her stuff because of what I had done. He reminds me every chance he can of my transgressions against her and God, as he calls them. I'd waited until he went to work and snuck into his bedroom where I figured he would have stuff of hers. Sure enough, the room had been full of paintings she'd done—all sceneries inspired by the area. My favorite had been one she'd painted of the nearby cornfields going on for miles. All I could think about at the time was how in the painting a person could get away from every-thing and everyone. And that's what I'd wanted. I wanted to get away from the town that knew me for an act I had no control over. I still want to get away. Because of me, an artist is gone forever, never to touch the world with her beauty.

Leon had returned and found me still admiring the cornfield painting. He'd dragged me from the room, twisting my arm so hard it hurt for days. I thought he was going to beat me; his body had trembled with anger when he threw me to the floor in my room. My pale skin had been covered in bruises I had to hide for weeks afterward. No one in the town does anything to stop him from hurting me; however, now it's only verbal abuse. He hasn't touched me since that day. But when he sees me in public, he rants and lets everyone within earshot know what kind of person I am.

I haven't been in Leon's bedroom since. He keeps it locked now. When my aunt died, everything she had that was my mother's, Leon took. I don't even have a picture of her.

My feet squish in my soaked sneakers as I make my way closer to the house. Tomorrow is going to suck for work. Thank goodness I wear different shoes for my job at the country club. Light from the TV flashes again and I see him passed out in the recliner in the living room. A bottle of whiskey on the table next to him. He's been drunk so much lately and his anger has gotten worse. At least he's passed out, though. I breathe a sigh of relief at not having to face him tonight. I only need a couple more days of work, then I'll get my final paycheck and be able to leave this place. I'm not giving anyone notice. I'll just go to the bus station and buy a ticket. I'm so glad my aunt had set me up a bank account before she died that Leon never knew about. I've been saving money to go to art school and get away from here. It's everything I have and all I've ever wanted.

I turn and make my way to the back of the property where a small shed Leon had built for my mother to paint sits. I found the key before he threw me out of the house; it's where I've been staying. There is no power, and I sleep in a sleeping bag on the floor with a comforter to keep myself warm in the colder weather. It's better than being homeless. No one in this town would help me if I asked. Unlocking the door, I make my way through the darkness. My eyes adjust and I quickly change out of my soaked clothes and shoes into a pair of sweatpants, a long T-shirt, and socks to sleep in. The chill in the air causes my skin to tingle, and I sigh at the thought of a warm shower at work tomorrow. I clean cabins at a local lakeside resort; they let me take a shower there in a room I need to clean. I dump my shoes upside down so the water inside can drain out. I won't have time tomorrow to stop at the local laundry mat to dry them for my walk home tomorrow night. I'll either have to wear my heels from my second job or the soaked shoes. I fall asleep thinking about my future and getting away from this damn town. Getting away from all the hate. You'd think Santa Claus, Indiana, a place where Christmas is celebrated year round, would be full of goodwill and support, but it's the complete opposite. I've never really felt at home here, because I've never really had a home. My aunt had tried, but Leon made sure to remind her at every turn that I didn't deserve one. I close my eyes and fall asleep quickly from exhaustion, and the nightmares come like they do every night.

Coal

Walking up to the car rental counter, I ask for any available SUV or all-wheel drive vehicle. The girl takes in my six-two frame and smiles. I smile back. I know I look good, but she does nothing for me. She's cute but in an overdone way. She's made up like she's going clubbing instead of working at an airport. Her uniform is standard car rental attire, but I can tell the manager has left for the day because the girl has undone quite a few buttons, exposing the tops of her breasts.

"I can show you to the local hotel." She offers as I sign the contract.

"Thank you, but I'm heading out of town." I slide the contract back, and she folds up my copies and slips them in an envelope. I watch as she writes the car information on the outside, but it's the phone number with hearts that causes me to grit my teeth.

"Well, if you change your mind…" She taps the phone number as she explains where the car is parked and the rules to refill it before returning it. I smile and turn away, pulling my duffle over my shoulder. I head for the exit hating that I'm back here again. Granted, Louisville isn't my final destination, but it's close enough to my home.

Fuck, home.

I haven't thought about that word in eight years. I work, then I go to a small apartment I inhabit. But it isn't a home. There's a bed, a kitchen, TV, and my workout bench. I spend more time on base in the gym, or volunteering for every mission I can get on. Yeah, I could have stayed in the barracks, but I needed to get away from other people. I wanted my own space. No, I needed my own space.

I walk up to the large white SUV; it's bigger than my Jeep Rubicon back in Nevada, but it'll do. After I throw my duffle onto the passenger seat and adjust the driver's seat to my taller frame, I set off toward the last place I want to be.

The drive from Louisville to Santa Claus, Indiana, takes just over an hour. I don't have to meet the attorney until four this afternoon at the Christmas Lake Golf Course clubhouse. It's about two in the afternoon now and I decide to drive around town getting to know it again. I expected changes, but I did not expect the large theme and water park combo. I turn down North Holiday Boulevard, passing the American Legion, and see the campgrounds my father has owned since I was a small boy. They have a light show celebrating Rudolph now. I shake my head. What happened to the town I knew?

The town is now ready for the Christmas season every day of the year regardless of the weather. I continue down the boulevard, passing a new doctor's office, and take a left as the memories hit me. My mom's gallery is just down the way. But as I get a look at the large parking lot with the post office, visitors bureau, and a small mall, I pull over and find a spot to park. I grab my mid-thigh length, wool black trench coat off the passenger seat and step out of the SUV. The temperature is cooler than what I'm used to in the desert. I put my coat on and pull it tight over my white button-down shirt to cut the chill.

Walking across the lot, I see the Ace Hardware store and a new boutique. I continue through the bank parking lot past them. There sitting like a lonely sentry is the small cottage shop my mother used to work out of. I jog up the stairs and walk across the porch to the front windows. The memories flash behind my eyes. I can almost see her standing there surrounded by artwork. She took such pride in the fact she was giving the locals a place to sell their wares. Sheets now cover easels and dust covers everything.

"Hey, man, that place isn't open," a voice says from behind me. I turn around and see a gangly teenage boy. He's in torn jeans that barely fit him, hanging lower than they should be.

"Pull your pants up." I order the kid. "I know it's not open."

"Mr. Bah Humbug doesn't like people on this porch." The kid smarts off, standing tall and letting his pants slide down more.

I want to chuckle at the nickname because that is exactly what my father is like.

"Yeah, well, let him come tell me himself." I move toward the stairs. The boy takes me in more before throwing down the skateboard in his hand and taking off across the parking lot. "Pull up your pants, punk," I holler at his back.

My phone vibrates from my pocket and I slip it out.

"Bridger," I growl into the phone as I watch the teenager skate past another teen, who he smacks in the head and says something that I can't make out. "Mother fucker," I exclaim, forgetting the phone is in my hand.

"Coal, are you there?"

"Yeah, sorry, Lee," I say to my family's attorney. "This town has changed a lot."

"You're here already? Where are you?"

"My mom's gallery." I look up at the sign and see it's covered. It no longer says CHRISTMAS WITH ELOISE ART STUDIO. I miss her standing here in what was her space.

"I'll meet you there," Lee says and hangs up.

I look back across the way to see the two punk teens, and as they go past me, a small woman with green eyes captures my attention. She turns to look at me before her hood obscures her face and she's off. Her eyes were so bright it was like looking into the green lights of a Christmas tree, but without the joy. I watch her as she heads out. A part of me wants to follow her, but there is nothing in this town I want or need. I make my way back up onto the porch and wait for the attorney.

As I look out across the parking lot toward the trees, I remember running through those woods as a kid. Then when I was a teenager, I would ride my bike from the high school to my mom's gallery to help her out. Earl, my father, was very rarely around growing up. He was out making money by buying more and more property and having it zoned for business. He owns this whole area I'm standing in. I wouldn't be surprised if he owned that amusement park or sold his land to the owners to build on.

I try not to think of the last time I talked to him. It was right after I turned eighteen. My mother had died the month before my birthday; she would still be alive if Earl had been home when she fell. But he was out with whatever secretary or club house-wife was the flavor of the month. I had told him I'd never forgive him, and he'd told me to get out. Not a problem. I'd walked to the nearest Air Force recruiting office and enlisted. I'm now a para-jumper living my life the way I want. I don't depend on his money for anything. I haven't been back to this town until now when Lee called me yesterday and woke me up. Earl died, and I needed to come back to take care of matters.

I'm shaken from my thoughts as Lee approaches. He's worked for my family since he got out of law school, a job he fell into because of his father who worked for my family as well. Now Lee is completely in charge of all legal matters regarding the Bridger family. Even though I've been estranged from my father, I still talk to Lee regularly. He has less hair than the last time I saw him, with more gray to the brown, but he still has the same smile.

"Coal, how are you doing, kid?" He holds out his hand for me to shake. I take it and my large hand swallows his thinner one. "Well, guess not a kid anymore." He chuckles.

"Hello, Lee." I smile at him and nod toward the door of my mother's gallery, praying he'll unlock it. Shortly after her death, Earl locked it and wouldn't let me in. With him gone now, I'm hoping I can get whatever I can before it's given to whomever Earl made his heir.

"Let me get the right key."

My foot shakes and I crack my knuckles as I impatiently wait while he goes through a huge key chain.

"Ah, got it, but there is no hurry to get in here." He turns to look at me.

"Yes, there is. I want her stuff before the heir gets it."

"Heir?" Lee's brows shoot up. "Coal, you're his heir. Didn't you get his letter?"

"What letter?" My father never tried to reach out to me after I left.

"Coal, you get everything. All the money, land, and so much more."

"Why?"

"Come in and let's talk, then I'll take you to the house."

"I know where the house is."

"He sold the old place and had a home built that overlooks the lake."

"I don't understand any of this." I look around my mother's gallery and notice that nothing has been touched in all these years. Just the sheets covering the paintings that she personally owned. I walk back to her office ignoring the pictures of her with students and artists on the wall, not ready to deal with those memories. When I enter her office, I find it's the only thing that's different. The desk is bare and the walls are clean of everything. It's like she was erased from here.

"Where is her stuff? When was her desk cleaned off?" I growl as I turn to look at Lee. He's only a couple inches shorter than me, but he steps back from the look in my eyes.

"After you left, your father came in and had everything boxed up. Last I heard, he had it put in storage for you."

"He told me I couldn't have anything. None of it. None of her stuff."

"Coal, come out here." Lee holds out his hand, directing me back to the main area.

"No, just tell me."

"I can't, son, you need to meet me at this address, then we can talk."

I ignore his "son" comment; I haven't been anyone's son in a long time. I take the offered card from him. When I get back to the SUV, I enter the address in the GPS and realize it's an address not far away on Candy Cane Lane. I head that way and wonder what the hell Earl had been thinking. My mother had always wanted a house on the lake, and I'm confused as I pull up in front of the large Victorian inspired home. The house sits atop a rolling grass hill with a large circular driveway and wrap around deck. The pillars of the deck are white, and the house is a beautiful deep green with white trim.

There is a large circular room on the second floor with big windows facing the lake. I step on the porch and look across the street to the lake and all the other houses lining the other side of it. This is exactly what my mom would have wanted.

Why did Earl build this home?

Lee pulls up and parks behind me in the driveway. I notice a second driveway that must lead to the garage, but I'm too busy trying to process everything to check. He pulls out a key and unlocks the big ornate door with frosted glass. It opens into a foyer with a chandelier hanging overhead. I step into the home and instantly smell my mother's favorite flowers and the stupid air freshener scents she loved. There are open doors to my right and left, and a large wooden circular staircase in front of me. Everything is styled as if my mother had done it herself. I stop in what must be the den. A large painting hangs over the marble fireplace. It was one of my mom's favorites. Tears clog my throat as the memories overtake me. I sit down on the light gray leather side chair.

"What is this place?" I choke on the words.

"Your father had it built five years ago. He moved out of your old home shortly after you left. Had it demolished and lived at one of the cabins at the campground until this place was done. He said the least he could do was give you a home your mother would be proud of." He smiles as he looks around, and I can see his eyes are misty too.

"What aren't you telling me, Lee?"

"After you left, he got the results of your mother's autopsy. He knew you blamed him for her death; he blamed himself too. But there is so much you don't know, Coal. You judged him for things your mother told him to do."

My eyes flare wide and I stand up and pace the room. "She was okay with her husband sleeping with whomever he wanted, even her friends?"

"Yes." I can't believe that. I need to get out of here. "Coal," he says as I turn to leave. "They had arrangements. Including the fact he could sleep with others. She had the one thing she wanted from him—you. They were friends, not lovers. He left you a letter explaining all of this. When you're ready, you should read it. But the thing you need to know is your mother was dead before her body hit the floor. She had an aneurysm."

His words stun me.

"Come on. I'll buy you a drink. But know this house is yours. Earl slept in a guest bedroom. He wanted you to move into this home and never think it was his. He never cheated on your mother after her death. He was faithful to his best friend. He regretted, just like you, that he wasn't home when she died."

He leads me out of the home, locking it behind him, and then to his car after he gives me the key to the house.

CHAPTER 2
KIERA

I pull the bike I found sitting waiting for me after I got off my shift cleaning cabins. It was Mr. Bridger's last gift to me. He died yesterday. After I got the news, I sat in the cabin he used to live in and cried. He was the only person in this awful town that was nice to me. He had helped me get the job at the country club dining room after I worked for him a bit. He was always mean to everyone but me. Everyone in town called him Mr. Bah Humbug; I called him Mr. Bridger. He would always take the time to talk to me, and he never called me names. He had once told me about his wife's old art gallery. When I road past it today, there was a man sitting on the porch. I'm wondering if now that Mr. Bridger is gone if it's for sale.

As I enter the women's locker room, I make my way to my locker and notice the lock has been broken again. I take a big breath and look around. I don't know why they insist on doing this, but I learned not to hide anything in my in my locker. The manager has been trying to fire me since she had to hire me. She's one of the townspeople that calls me names behind my back and to my face. Her latest is to call me a criminal, and that's why she keeps busting into my locker. I grab my clothes and step into one of the stalls to change. I never change in front of people; they don't need to know how much their words hurt me. As I slide my jeans down my legs, my fingers brush the scars on the outside of my thighs, and I calm instantly just touching them. I haven't harmed myself in a long time, not since I've learned techniques to better deal with my emotions, like my body art. The beautiful flowers lining my thighs down to my calves comfort me. Some of the artwork faded today when I took a shower, but I'll do more tonight to get over the nerves from today. Losing Mr. Bridger is just another reason I have to get out of this godforsaken town.

I slide my pressed black slacks up my legs and slip my black shirt on over my bra, then I step out of the stall. I free my dark hair from the ponytail it has been in since my shower. My hair is so thick it's still damp. I brush it out before styling it into a low bun at the back of my neck. I line my eyes with black eyeliner and put on a little blush and mascara.

My fair skin is flawless, and I don't need powder or foundation like several of the other girls that work here. My aunt always told me I had skin like my mother's. I sit on the bench and slip on the required black low heel dress shoes, then I put on the dark gray tie and matching sleeve armbands. The armbands make us look like dealers at a casino. Rounding out my work uniform is the long, black waist apron with the country club logo in the center.

"Hey, freak, you have the window section. A two top just walked in," my manager barks at me.

"Yes, ma'am." I nod as I step through the swinging doors and pull out my notepad.

As I approach the table of two men, one turns to look at me, and I recognize him as the man that was standing outside Eloise's gallery. His blue eyes zero in on me and trace me from my shoes to the top of my head. I try not to trip and embarrass myself when it feels like a caress to my skin. As I get closer to him, he leans back, and his white button-down pulls tight across his muscular arms. The cuffs are rolled up, exposing a tattoo on his right arm that runs from his wrist up under the sleeve of his shirt. I step up to the table and he stands; I'm a tall girl at five foot seven, but I need to tip my head back to look up at his over six-foot height.

"Hello, Kiera, did you get the gift left for you this morning?" a voice says, intruding on the staring contest I have going with the tall stranger. His body is so big, and the smell of his cologne is just faint enough that I want to lean in and smell him more. "Kiera?" the voice says again, and I turn to look at the stranger's companion.

My fears about Eloise's place being for sale are confirmed when I see Mr. Bridger's attorney sitting there.

"Oh, hello, Mr. Rumble. I'm sorry, what did you say?" I stutter as the large man steps closer to me. I slip my notepad into my pocket as I turn back to him. His dark hair is cut close to his head on the sides and a bit longer on the top. His cheeks fill as he smiles down at me, revealing a dimple on his left side. Holy shit, this guy is seriously hot.

"I asked if you got the gift I left for you." At Mr. Rumble's comment, something clouds over the hot guy's eyes. He swings around to look at him and then back to me. A growl escapes his throat, and with that sound, my instincts kick in and I step back, protecting myself. The hot guy starts to step toward me.

"Coal, have a seat, let Kiera do her job."

"What is she to you?" The hot guy's voice is rough sounding but husky, causing parts of my body to quaver and my heart to slam into my chest.

"She is a friend."

Coal looks between us again.

"You said you left her a gift?" He reaches out and grabs my forearm. His grip isn't tight or bruising, but the contact is causing my heart to beat even faster.

"Is there a problem over here?" My manager approaches us.

"Oh, no, Barbie. No problem. Coal just wanted me to introduce him to Kiera." Mr. Rumble stands up.

My heart is completely beating out of my chest now. Both men are taller than me, and the little voice in my head is demanding I run. That I get away and protect myself.

"Oh, Mr. Bridger." Barbie gasps as she takes in Coal. He's still holding on to my arm, and I start to pull away. His hand slides down my arm and takes my hand in his, holding me tight. I try to shake him off.

"I'll get you water." I push the words past my thick tongue, needing a moment.

"Yes, get them water." Barbie directs me. Again, I try to pull away from Coal, but he holds my hand tight. "Mr. Bridger, please let her do her job."

"I didn't get to introduce myself." He turns toward me, and his blue eyes darken as he looks at me. "I'm Coal Bridger."

"Kiera." I drop my gaze so I can't see the intensity of his. "Nice to meet you."

I step away and make my escape as soon as he releases my hand. I grab a pitcher of water and two glasses that weren't on their table. Barbie walks past me, bumping my shoulder and causing water to slosh out of the pitcher and on to my shoes and sleeve. I grit my teeth and make my way back toward the table. I focus on where I'm walking but I can feel Coal's eyes on me as I approach. He doesn't take them off me while I pour water for Mr. Rumble.

"To answer your question, Mr. Rumble, yes, I got Mr. Bridger's gift. Thank you." I nod at him and turn to Coal. I focus on the table instead of him as I fill his glass. He clears his throat, and I move my eyes up to his after I set his water down. "I'm sorry for your loss, Mr. Bridger. Your father was a very nice man; he'll be missed."

"You're the only person other than Lee who

thinks Earl was nice. What did he do for you?" He growls again, and I step back and retrieve my notepad.

"What can I get you gentlemen tonight?"

"Kiera, I'll have a scotch neat, please. Tell whoever's at the bar, top shelf. Same for Coal here. Also, get him the prime rib special, medium rare. I won't be staying for dinner."

"Mr. Bridger, mashed or baked potato? Seasonal veggies or salad?" I ask the questions for the sides. "Would you like a different drink with your dinner?"

"Baked with butter and sour cream. Salad, ranch on the side, no croutons. I'll have water with my meal," he says, his eyes taking me in again.

"I'll get your orders entered. Another server will bring your drinks."

"No," Coal says. "I want you to serve me." My spine straightens. Does he like people to serve him? Does he have the ego others accused his father of having, which I never saw?

"I can't bring you your alcohol order," I say and storm off.

Coal

I watch my little pixie walk away from me. Her body is slim, almost to the point of unhealthy. I want to make her sit down and eat the meal with me. When I had her hand in mine, I wanted to pull her into me. I wanted to mark her as mine so everyone would know. But her trembling body told me someone has scared my pixie. I'll protect her with everything I am.

My pixie?

Where the hell did that come from? Something about her calls to a part of me I have never felt before. Her body isn't curvy, and it's completely covered, unlike her manager, who has her cleavage on full display. But I could see her tight ass through the slacks that molded to her.

"Coal, Kiera is only eighteen; she can't serve alcohol to us." Lee's voice breaks through my thoughts.

Eighteen! Legal. I want her, and I will do everything I can to have her.

Another server walks up to our table, this one in tighter black slacks, impractical high heels, and her breasts straining against the tight white button-down shirt. The top few buttons are undone, and her gray tie is loose around her neck. Kiera's uniform was perfectly pressed and completely practical, down to her shoes with a low heel. It's the illusion of what is under her clothes that is the sexiest for her.

"Mr. Bridger, can I get you anything else?" The server purrs, and I curtly tell her no. I look across the table to Lee again.

"Tell me about Kiera and my father?" Something bitter enters my throat at that thought. What is their connection? My father was nice to her. He got her gifts. Were they involved?

"Your father took a shine to Kiera after she started working at the cabins cleaning them. Something about her mother being a friend to your mom. Plus, most people around here don't like Kiera." He raises his brow in question, and I can tell we're thinking the same thing.

Why don't they like her?

I watch as Kiera floats through the dining room serving others. She smiles but it never reaches her eyes. It's as if she is sad all the time. She avoids looking at our table, and I want her undivided attention on me. When she delivered my salad, she took another drink order from me. But Lee wanted to talk about my mother's gallery, which kept me from talking to Kiera. Plus, she had food for other tables to deliver. I can see the small muscles in her arms flex beneath her sleeves.

Lee and I discuss meeting up on Monday to sign papers. Before he takes off, he lets me know a cab will take me back to the house. As he walks out, Kiera makes her way toward me with a large tray on her shoulder. She's weaving around everyone with ease. She passes me to grab a stand that she kicks open before setting her tray down. I notice only my food is on her tray.

"Can I ask you a question?" I lean back with my hands resting on my stomach, fingers laced so I don't reach out and grab her again. Her eyes roam my body and I'm instantly turned on. The shock to my system the first time I touched her was bigger than the adrenaline rush I get when I jump out of airplanes.

She pauses and looks at me. "Yes, sir."

"Do I scare you?"

Her pulse picks up in her delicate throat, and she swallows. I can almost hear the thoughts going through her head as she contemplates my question.

"No, sir. I'm just doing my job. Can I get you anything else?"

"What gift did my father give you?" I want her to stay and visit with me. I don't want her to rush off. I've never felt like this with a woman. My relationships with women are limited to one-night stands, just someone to help me relieve myself. Anything more than that would mean opening my heart to losing them too.

"He gave me a bicycle. He tried to give me a car a few months ago, but I refused to take it. He didn't like that I walk or run everywhere. He was afraid I'd be hit by a car in the dark on our country roads." She stops when she realizes how much she shared with me.

She doesn't have a car. She walks, or now bikes, everywhere.

"Doesn't your family come to get you? Why would he help you?" My little pixie drops her eyes, and I know she's about to lie to me when her body tenses.

"They are too busy. Your father was just nice to me. He never told me why, other than he knew my mother. It started when I was fourteen and I got a job at the cabins. I went to clean a cabin he was staying in and he started talking to me."

"Who is your mom?" I wonder if she was one

of Earl's many conquests and Kiera is a sibling of mine.

"She died a long time ago. I need to get back to work," she says, her voice barely a whisper as she steps away.

"Wait, can you get me another drink?" She nods, and I watch her head toward the bar. She places the order then goes to help the busboy clear other tables. After about ten minutes of me eating and looking out over the rolling hills of the golf course, I think about the house Earl built for me. I'm confused as to why he would do that. And why he would help Kiera. What was he doing? It's as if he was trying to change who he was in the past by doing good things before his death, making amends.

"Is there anything else I can get for you?" I look up into the window and see her reflection as she takes me in. When I turn to look at her directly, she tips her head down again. She avoids looking at me.

"I'd like another drink." My buzz is in full force because I started drinking on an empty stomach, but I don't have to drive. Drowning in a little alcohol could numb this pain in my chest. Another two or three can't hurt. "Also, what's good on the dessert menu?" I push back my plate with only half my potato left and my meat all gone.

"The chef makes a delicious fried ice cream, and we have New York style cheesecake, and a variety of pies made from locally grown fruit," she says as she pulls out her notepad and pen. "What would you like?"

"Which do you like?" She shifts her feet and her eyes flash up to mine. It's like no one has ever asked her that question before. She is finally giving me attention though, so I don't question it. "Well, what would you eat? On your birthday, what do you get?" I ask when she doesn't respond. Her little tongue slips out and licks her top lip as if she is imagining something good. My cock jumps in my jeans, and I can just picture her licking my dick with that tongue. I try not to adjust myself right there in front of her, and I groan when her eyes glass over. I know it's not from desire, but God, I want her to have that look for me.

"I'd have the crème brûlée with strawberries on top." She sighs.

"I'll have two of those."

"Two?"

"Yes. I don't want to share mine with you." I smile at her. Her lips kick up on one side.

"I can't eat while I work."

"When's your break?"

Her eyes drop again. "I'll get you your dessert and place the order for your drink."

I grab for my water and shake the glass so she can see it's empty. She nods as she turns and walks away from me again. I'm going to get that little pixie to have a bite of that dessert if it's the last thing I do.

I'm imagining her opening her pillowing lips, and her pink tongue sliding along the spoon as I slip it into her mouth. I adjust myself when I hear a gasp. I look up to see the server from the bar with my drink.

"Thank you," I growl, and take the glass from her hand and down it. "Get me another."

"Sure, handsome." She bats her lashes at me. From this distance I can tell they're fake. She returns to the bar, and I look around for Kiera but don't see her anywhere. Where is my dessert? After a moment, the server returns with a tray. She gives me a sly smile as she hands me my next drink, then she sets both of my crème brûlées down.

"Where is Kiera?" I ask with a bite to my words.

"I'm going to take care of you for the rest of your visit." She holds the tray against the side of her body and wiggles her hips.

"No. I want Kiera to finish helping me." I stand so fast that my chair falls back, and I grip the table when I start to sway. Okay, maybe I shouldn't have ordered more drinks. I swing my head around, looking for my pixie. "Kiera," I yell across the room, hoping she'll come out of hiding. I don't know what I said to scare her off, and she didn't tell me she was going on break or leaving.

"Um, can I help you, Coal?" The manager walks up to my table again.

"My name is Mr. Bridger, or Staff Sergeant Bridger to you." I drop my rank hoping to intimidate her. "Where is Kiera? She was serving me, and I wasn't done talking to her." I step forward, trying to move to where I've watched Kiera go when she heads to the back. My legs wobble. Fuck, too much alcohol, and now she's escaped me because I wasn't paying attention. I was slacking again. I need to find her before she's taken from me too. Pain seizes my chest at the thought.

"Mr. Bridger, sit down. We will get you some coffee and Deana here will finish serving you."

"I said no. Where is Kiera?" I growl in the manager's face. She steps back, her eyes widening in fear.

"What's the big deal with the freak?" Deana mumbles, and I swing around to look at her.

"What did you call my Kiera?" I start to step toward her but she runs off.

"Mr. Bridger, Ms. Joyner is no longer on the premises." The manager distracts me from going after the other server.

"Where did she go?"

"I told her to leave. She is no longer employed with us."

"Put everything on my tab." I push past her and storm out of the room. I grab my jacket from the coat check and slip it on, then I slam open the doors and head into the night. The valet jumps when the door hits the wall. "Call me a cab." I don't know where my pixie has gone, but I start looking around. I see a dark form swing onto a bike near the edge of the building, and I'm off. I run toward her hoping I'm right. I grab her arm and pull her off the bike and against my chest. She yelps and starts fighting me.

"Pixie, it's me," I say, and she starts to calm. "Why did you leave me?" I calm too when I have her where I need her. She's safe.

When she turns around, she sniffles and squares her shoulders. Her eyes are brighter in the dim light, but I can't make out very much more than that.

"I need to go," she says as she tries to pull away from me.

"You're coming with me." I pull her closer to me with one hand while using the other to pull her bike along with us, making her walk with me back to the entrance where a cab is now waiting. "Get in, now." I demand, and she slips into the back seat. I push the bike to the trunk, and the driver comes around to help me secure it in there with a cord.

When I slide in next to her, I grip her thigh, pulling her closer to me as I give the driver my address.

"Why are you doing this?" Her question stops me, and I turn to look at her.

"When we get to the house, we can talk, pixie. When was the last time you ate?" I take her in more and remember how thin she looked. She's now dressed in jeans that are ripped up like people pay for, but I can tell hers aren't store-bought. The softness of the denim against the palm of my hand tells me hers are worn. Her jacket isn't very thick, and I start to slip off my coat to put around her shoulders when she trembles. "You're freezing."

"No. I'm fine." She puts her hand on my chest.

I stop what I'm doing and reach down to lace my fingers with hers and raise her hand to my mouth. I kiss her delicate wrist, her fingers freezing cold against my skin. I grab her other hand and wrap my hands around them, holding them tight to warm them up.

"Pixie, where are your gloves?"

Her eyes drop and I lift her chin so I can look in her eyes in the darkness. I want to kiss her. I lean forward, and just as my lips are about to press to hers, my eyes cross and everything goes dark.

CHAPTER 3
KIERA

Coal's head falls against me, banging into my forehead, and his body goes lax. He passed out on me. I was about to be kissed for the first time, and now he's out cold. Shoot. I don't know where we are going, or why he wanted me to go with him. All I know is that with his body next to mine, I've never felt this safe and warm. My body feels alive as the hair along my arm stands on end. His breath against my face makes me realize how close I was to feeling intimacy for the first time. But now I'm left feeling needy and desiring his touch.

I look out the windshield as I wrestle Coal's big body to lay back. I recognize where we are just as the cab turns up the circular driveway. I've been here many times. I clean here on the weekends; I even helped with decorating the place. In the garage is the brand new, bright red Lincoln MKX Mr. Bridger gave me. I cried when he gave it to me because I knew I couldn't keep it. He didn't know I was leaving town. I couldn't tell him, and I wouldn't take the car with me. That would be wrong. But no one has ever helped me like he did or cared about me like that since my aunt died.

When the cab comes to a stop, I shake Coal awake. He grumbles and pulls out some bills to pay the driver then stumbles out of the cab. I get my bike from the trunk and I'm about to take off and leave when I turn to see Coal trip on the porch. I push the bike up the stairs and set it against the bench on the porch.

Helping Coal to his feet, I take the keys from him to open the door and help him into the foyer. His big body dwarfing mine, I can barely hold him up. But everywhere he touches me tingles. He leans down and kisses my hair, and I hear him inhale as if he's smelling me. I want to pull away but more importantly, I want to melt into him. Let him teach me passion and caring for only one night.

"God, you smell so good. Come on, pixie." He slurs next to my ear and my breath catches when I feel his tongue lick the shell. I wonder why he keeps calling me that. He pulls away and grips my hand as he drags me up the marble and wood circular staircase. I'm afraid he's going to fall when he stumbles a few times, but he keeps his feet under him and keeps us moving up the stairs. When we reach the top, he spins around looking at all the doors and halls leading off the landing. "Um?" His brows drop in confusion.

"Are you looking for your room?" I ask him.

"I don't have a room here," he says, starting toward the open area in front of us that looks down into the family room.

"Your room is this one." I turn to my left and point at the double doors that lead into the master bedroom.

"How do you know?" He slurs again as he pushes the doors open, dragging me behind him.

"I clean the house on the weekends for your father." I stop. "I mean, I used to clean for him."

He takes in the room and walks over to the large platform bed with a heavy wooden head-board. My hand is still firmly in his grip. The room is decorated in browns, whites and grays. The round sitting area off to the side reminds me of a turret you'd find in a castle. There are two in the house, the first being here in the master, and the other across the house. The second one isn't deco-rated but I always imagined it as the perfect art studio because it overlooks the lake and valley in the distance. The house is perfect and a testament to Mr. Bridger's love for his son and deceased wife. I could never understand why Coal avoided coming back here. I would spend all my time in this house trying to make it a home. It was the only decorating I couldn't do. How do you make a house a home?

On that thought, I need to get out of here before I think about Coal making this a home with someone else. Or worse, him selling it.

"Okay, so now that you're in your room and safe, I'll lock up on my way out." I try to pull my hand out of his to get away from him. My body has been on fire ever since we walked into the room. I've never wanted another person to touch me like I want him to touch me. I can even imagine him touching my scars and not being repulsed by them.

He pulls off his jacket, letting it fall to the floor as he lets go of my hand.

"Strip, pixie." He demands, and I step back finally feeling the fear I normally do around others.

"I'm not that kind of girl." My chin tips up as I stare him down, my voice sounding stronger than I feel. "I don't care what anyone told you, I don't sleep with random people."

He steps toward me, or more like stumbles toward me, and I step back again. My heart starts to crumble thinking he thought I was special but instead he just wants a quick fuck.

"Pixie." His voice is soft, and his eyes slide to the door. I see the instant he worries I'm going to flee. "I don't want that right now, because the first time my cock slides into your tight pussy, I'm going to be sober and you're not going to fear me. I just want to sleep with you against me. Please," he begs, and his words do something to me. My body reacts by causing moisture to gather between my thighs. I've never slept, just slept, with anyone. I've never done the other kind of sleeping—the sex kind—with anyone either. But just to be held... My aunt wasn't touchy feely like that. She would hug me, but she never curled up next to me in bed when I had a nightmare or when I would go to her. I swallow the thickness in my mouth as I wonder what it would feel like to just be held.

"Please, pixie." He moves to unbutton his shirt but instead rips the buttons off. His chest is bare of hair, and his muscles are defined, even the abs. A full six-pack. I want to trace them with my fingers.

"Okay," I say. It's just one night. I'm leaving town soon and I'm never going to get this chance again. Not with someone like him, or feeling like I do for him already. I lean down and untie my tennis shoes, and toe them off. I slip my jacket off and set it on a bench against the wall near the dressers. I look down to my hoodie and jeans unsure of how much to take off, so I unbutton my jeans because they won't be comfortable to sleep in. The room is dim enough he won't see my scars. I slide the jeans down my legs and bend over slightly when I hear a groan. I spin around to see him standing in only a pair of tight, black boxer briefs. His impressive erection peeks out the top band. He adjusts himself as he stares at me openly. I look down worried he sees something he doesn't like.

"Fuck, pixie, those sexy panties are going to make me come."

I look back at him in confusion; I'm wearing plain, white cotton panties. I take in the intricate tattoo climbing up his right arm onto his chest. The skulls and warriors with swords are in black and causes his already muscular arms to stand out more. On his left arm is a military tattoo with what looks like a parachute and an angel. His legs are long and defined with muscles like I've never seen. Even his feet are sexy. My breathing increases as I watch him adjust himself again.

"Take off the sweatshirt, Kiera." His gruff voice breaks me from my perusal of his body.

I slip the ragged sweatshirt off. My white bra with lace around the edges is almost too small to contain my now fuller B size breasts. His eyes take me in, and I've never felt sexier in my life. He walks toward me and this time I don't step back. He stops close to me and lifts his hand out, palm up. I look down at it and slip my hand into his. His fingers lace with mine and he pulls me to the edge of the bed. He's not going to last much longer by the way he's swaying on his feet. He drops my hand and runs both his hands into my hair. I'd pulled my hair free after I changed out of my work uniform. His strong fingers rub my scalp as he manipulates my head back. I look up at him and bite my bottom lip.

"I'm going to kiss you, Kiera, and that's all. Then you're going to climb into this bed and let me hold you for the night."

I sigh and nod my head.

He leans down and his lips feather across mine; my eyes slip closed. He pulls away but still right there. I slip my tongue out to taste him, and my eyes flare open wide at the groan that rips from his chest. He slams his lips back onto mine. This time there is nothing soft and gentle about the kiss. It's demanding, claiming, needy. I moan as the heat from his lips overcomes mine. I open when his tongue presses against my lips. His tongue enters and dominates my mouth, touching every part. He groans as his hands leave my hair and move to my hips to pull me up to him. My feet leave the floor as he stands to his full height. On instinct, I wrap my legs around his hips, and I feel his erection at the juncture of my pussy. The heat of him against the wetness makes me rock against him. More wetness seeps from my body as his hands knead my ass. I moan into his mouth when I feel the bed against my back and him over the top of me. He rocks against me, and I rip my mouth from his as I cry out from the feeling of euphoria overcoming my body. Tingles erupt throughout me. I want more. I need more. Something is happening I've never felt before.

"I need...something," I beg him, unable to describe what it is I need.

"Fuck, pixie. I need to be inside you, but I don't want to right now. I'm too drunk and don't want to hurt you." His hand leaves my ass and slides into my panties. He brushes a finger against me, and I arch my body, needing more. "You're so fucking wet for me." He circles my clit and the euphoric feelings climb higher and higher. My body tightens like a coil, and when he slips a long finger into me as his thumb continues to rub my clit, I orgasm screaming his name. He removes his hand and presses his still covered cock against me. He throws his head back and groans as I feel moisture between both of us. He rolls off my body and collapses next to me.

"Coal?" I turn and find his eyes are closed. I think he's just trying to catch his breath but then a loud snore breaks the quiet. "Well, shoot." I look down both our bodies and see his cum wetting his boxers, and I'm not sure what to do. Do I clean him up? I don't want to seem like a creeper. I've never done this before.

I slip from the bed and go to the attached bathroom where I get a washcloth and clean myself. I walk back out to the bedroom and wonder if I should leave, but I told him I'd stay. So I walk back over to the bed and slip under the covers after I cover him with the blanket folded at the bottom of the bed. I fall asleep pressed against him. His warmth and the softness of the bed comfort me like I've never felt before.

Coal

. . .

A soft body presses against mine. A warmth I haven't felt in a long time seeps into my heart. The smell of soft vanilla overcomes my senses and the image of a green-eyed pixie with long brown hair and a body that sets me on fire fills my head. My eyes flash open and I see the sun starting to rise through the curtains. I pull Kiera in tighter to me as she nestles into me.

The memories of last night flood my mind. What she felt like on my fingers. Her face as she orgasmed. I'd felt the evidence of her virginity as my finger was buried in her. I can't wait to make her mine. My morning wood presses into her tight ass and I feel the crusty remnants of my orgasm. I extricate myself from her body and look around the room. My bag is downstairs, so I make my way into the adjoining bathroom, where I clean myself, take care of the morning breath, and slip on the large fluffy robe on the back of the door. I walk down the stairs to grab my bag, then head back up to the room. I plan to wake Kiera with my mouth on that virgin pussy of hers, but I find the bed empty.

My eyes flash around the room and I spot her slipping into her jeans as she talks on the phone. Her eyes are staring back at me.

"I'll be there in thirty minutes," she says to the

person on the other end of the line. She's going to leave me.

I'm across the room in no time, my long legs eating up the distance. I pull the phone from her ear, and she squeals when I pick her up. I pull her back against my chest and hear the person on the phone holler her name.

"Who is this?" I demand into the phone.

"This is Penny at Santa Claus Christmas store. Who am I speaking to?"

"This is Coal Bridger; Kiera won't be in today." I hang up the phone and drop it onto the floor by her shoes.

Turning, I make my way to the bed and toss her onto it. I'm on her, ripping her jeans and panties off, before she even bounces. I bury my face in her core and she cries out. She tries to push me away, but I need her taste on my tongue. She stops fighting at the first lick and arches her back. I wrap my arms around her thighs, opening her up more to me and holding her down so I can do what I planned to do.

"I wanted to wake you up with my mouth, and you ruined that. Now you're going to take my tongue until you beg me for more," I say against her core. She writhes above me, and I look up her slender body to see her green eyes hooded and looking down at me. Her teeth bite into her lip to keep her from crying out.

I leisurely drag my tongue through her folds as I push into her, and fuck her with it like my cock will be doing soon. I press my demanding cock into the bed, trying to keep myself in control.

She cries out as her body bows, her knees trying to close but I'm stronger. She shoves her hands into my short hair and pulls me in tighter as I continue to use my tongue to fuck her. She moves around, trying to get off, but I'm keeping her right on the cusp, just like she left me all last night while I watched her serving others. She had taken care of them like she should have been paying attention to me. When her head starts thrashing around, that's my cue to give her more.

I move to her clit and circle it as it comes out of its hood. I slide one finger into her tightness, then a second, and I curl my fingers to rub her G-spot. When I suck the little bud into my mouth, she screams, and her legs lock, her whole body spasms.

"Give me one more, pixie, then I'll give you my cock. Your little virgin pussy is begging for me to own it. Mark it as mine." The words cause my own cock to leak precum as it wants inside of her.

I focus on her pussy completely, sucking the lips and circling her clit over and over as I continue to finger fuck her. I reach up her body and pull down her bra cups, exposing her tits. They fit my hand perfectly. Her dusky nipples stand erect, demanding attention. I slide up her body, my fingers still in her heat. I nip her trim stomach, and when I'm over her breasts, I take a nipple into my mouth. My free hand tries to take my robe off. She sees me struggling and helps me get out of it. When I switch breasts, her pussy ripples around my fingers and her body bows under me again. I pull away to watch her, needing to see her orgasm. Her beauty before me takes my breath away. She stretches her arms above her, reaching for the headboard. I see small thin scars on the inside of her upper arms and for a moment I pause what I'm doing, trying to justify what I'm seeing. When she screams my name again and grows slicker as she orgasms, I pull my fingers out and suck them into my mouth, cleaning every bit of her off so I'm taking it into me.

Lining my aching, dripping cock up with her entrance, I slowly slide into her, knowing she's a virgin and not caring if she's on birth control. I push until I get to her hymen.

"I'll make it good for you, pixie." I look down at her as I try to hold myself from slamming into her.

"Coal, I need you. Only you. No one else." Her words settle something soul deep in me.

I press through and pull out before I push all the way in. My cock is so deep inside her I can feel myself right up against her cervix. I hold myself there while she adjusts to me. When I feel her muscles go lax, I pull out and start to move like my body demands.

I move up to my knees and pull her body up with me. She's over the top of my thighs and I reach around her to unhook her bra and toss it away. Every part of our naked bodies that can are touching. The need to imprint her on me and me on her overcomes me, and I lean down, marking her breast with a love bite. She throws her head back as she moves over me. My hands gripping her hips slam her down on me harder. Every slide of my cock against her tight walls causes my balls to pull up. I lay her back on the bed and start moving harder into her body, chasing the orgasm that is tingling along my spine. She cries out, her body bowing, her breasts jiggling, and I need her closer. I drop down and cage her body in. My arms wrap under her torso and over her shoulders for leverage as I go deeper.

"Coal. Oh God, Coal! I feel you everywhere," she cries out and my hips pump harder until she screams. Her neck flexes, her body trembles. My body locks up and I come, splashing deep inside her.

"You're mine now," I growl as my world crawls to a stop. My body falls toward hers, and at the last minute, I roll us so she's sprawled on top of me. I hold her tight to me not wanting to let her go.

CHAPTER 4
KIERA

I come awake wrapped in Coal's arms, our legs tangled together. There's an ache at my core that is slightly sore. His cock is still nestled inside my body, and as I move, I feel him lengthening inside me.

He groans and the rumble in his chest shakes me. I lean up, my hair falling around us in sheets blocking out the world around us. I look down into his blue eyes that remind me of the lake in the summertime. His thick, dark brows are relaxed. He's got a deep, dark five o'clock shadow. He's watching me, and as he shifts, his hips push his cock deeper. I bite my lip, his movement causing nerves that are raw to ache but also to beg for more.

"Let's take a shower, then I need to feed you, pixie." He smiles, his voice so husky sounding it turns me on. To my horror and embarrassment, I feel more moisture leak around us where we are still joined and his cum is leaking.

from me. "Kiera, I want you again, but I know you're going to be sore because I took you like a madman. Shower, food, then I'm going to fuck you on the counter in the kitchen."

I slide my palms up his chest and rise up, lodging his cock deeper inside me. The moan that comes from my throat surprises me. I slide up, then back down onto him.

I proceed to move my hips in slow, circular, and up and down movements. I'm not sure I'm doing it right, but when he grips my hips and yanks me down hard onto his pelvis and growls, I know I'm doing something right. He rolls us and proceeds to make love to me again, this time slower but still so deep I can feel him everywhere.

When we finally get out of bed, it's after noon. Like he promised, he washes every part of my body, including my sore core.

I try to wash him but he stops me. He says if I touch him, he'll be pressing me into the wall and fucking me into tomorrow. I smile and he shakes his head.

"Pixie, you are insatiable."

"But that sounds good. I've never had that done before."

"I'll fuck you into tomorrow once you're not hurting so much."

I need to talk to him about the fact we didn't use a condom. I bite the inside of my lip; I've never had this conversation before. As I'm about to broach the subject, his hands brush across the outside of my thighs and I see the moment he feels the scars. I pull away and jump from the shower and rush out of the room. I grab a towel on the way out, and I can feel his eyes following me. No one knows how low I got. How close I came to ending it. Subconsciously I cross my arms over my chest, my fingers play against the scars on the inside of my arms. I calm as soon as I feel them.

I stand there in the middle of the bedroom taking myself to that place where it's just me and the blood is sliding down my skin.

I'm ripped from my thoughts when his hands grip my hips and twist my body around. Again, I find myself flying through the air before landing on the bed. And again, his body is over the top of me, but this time he's not trying to make love to me. His face is tight. One of his big hands holds my arms over the top of my head. My weakness glaringly exposed.

"What the fuck are these marks, Kiera?" He

demands as his other hand traces the fine thin scars. Four on the inside of each arm. He pulls back and looks down my body seeing the four on the outside of each thigh.

I close my eyes and fight the tears back. He can't know what they are.

"Kiera." He chokes, and I realize my tears are slipping out uncontrolled.

"I'm broken." My lips tremble. "I need to punish myself." I say the words I've never told anyone else. My soul rips apart as he looks down at me and I can't hide what I am from him.

"Pixie, let me hold you together," he says against my lips, and gently kisses me. "Don't hurt yourself anymore. I need you." His words shock me. How can someone I just met feel so vital to me?

"I haven't done it in a while. Whenever I get the urge, I touch the old scars and it helps," I confess.

He kisses my forehead, each cheek, my nose, and then my lips again. He pulls away and kisses over every scar, licking them with his tongue, and instead of settling me like when I touch them myself does, I feel a fullness in my heart. A warmth I've never felt before. The need to be everything he needs overwhelms me.

"I promise if I feel the urge, I'll tell you," I

whisper as he takes my lips in a kiss that makes my toes curl. His tongue touching every part of my mouth, sliding against my own tongue, dancing.

He pulls back and both of us are breathless. His cock is heavy and erect between us.

"Food," he says as he pulls up, and my stomach growls.

I smile and hide my face away from him.

Something hits my legs and I look down to see a soft blue T-shirt. I slip it over my head and realize I don't have any panties or clean underclothes.

"Come on, pixie." He reaches out for me and I take his hand. The T-shirt is long and lands just above my knees, covering everything. We make our way downstairs and to the kitchen at the back of the house. He lifts me up onto the island, and I cringe when my butt hits the cold marble counter-top. He smiles as he turns and starts going through cupboards and the fridge.

"I made sure everything was fully stocked last weekend when I was here," I say, and he turns to look at me with a soft smile on his lips. I want that look on his face all the time. My heart thumps hard in my chest.

I watch as he prepares us omelets. No matter how many times I try to help him, he tells me to stay put. He hands me a plate with a large glass of milk, and I start eating. I didn't realize how famished I was. I haven't eaten since lunch yesterday.

When I'm finished and he takes my plate away from me, I try to jump down but he blocks me in and pushes me back to lie on the island. He lifts up my borrowed T-shirt and proceeds to use his mouth on me before he thrusts inside me again.

He makes love to me right there in the kitchen, then a second round on the floor in the family room. I'm so sore now and worried that my conversation with him is too late in coming. He's come inside me every time we've made love.

Now we are driving into town and I'm dressed in my jeans and clothes that we put through the wash before we left. He pulls up to the entrance of the Santa Claus Land of Lights, and I turn to him.

"Why are we here?"

"I haven't done this in years, and I want to do it with you. You're probably tired of seeing it, but where I live in Nevada there is no snow."

"I haven't gone through this since I was eleven." I smile at him.

When we'd finally left the house, it was lightly snowing.

We drive through the twelve miles of Christmas lights laughing, and Coal stops to take my picture every so often in front of different exhibits. I'm looking at this crazy, weird town through different eyes for the first time ever. When we finish and get back on the road, he drives toward the shopping center and post office. He pulls up in front of the gallery where I saw him for the first time. It doesn't feel like it was just yesterday. It feels like it was a life-time ago.

"The first time I laid eyes on you was right here, pixie."

"I was worried you were buying this place."

"I own it now. It's the only thing I have left of my mother. She loved art. She wasn't very good at it, but she could sell and show it like it was nothing. This gallery is everything to me. I couldn't sell it."

"Your mother sounds like she was an amazing woman."

"Come on." He doesn't say more but gets out of the SUV. I step out and walk to the front.

"Freak," is yelled, and I turn to see a group of people I graduated with standing outside the Subway restaurant.

"Shut the fuck up," Coal growls and starts walking toward them. I grab at his arm and pull him back.

"Ignore them," I beg.

"No. Why do they call you that?" His eyes bore into mine. I want to tell him. I want to confess my sins. Why this thing between us can only be this weekend. Why I'm leaving this town and going where no one will know what I've done. But I can't. The words are lodged in my throat.

"Please," I say again as tears spring to my eyes. I know if he really wanted to get by me he could.

"Hey, Bridger," a deep voice says from behind me.

Coal looks up and his body tenses. I turn around, keeping myself in front of him, and see the sheriff in his car. He looks at me and then across the parking lot to the group. Something crosses his face, and for a moment, I think it's pity. But no one in this town has ever pitied me. After Leon had told everyone what I did, I became the freak. I became —I can't even think the word. My body spasms in fear. Coal will leave me too when he finds out the truth.

"Hello, Kiera," Sheriff Kullen says in a softer voice.

"Sheriff." I nod at him.

"Hugh, is that you?" Coal says from behind me. He locks his arm around me and walks us toward the car. My body is tight against his, and the sheriff looks between us.

"Hey there," they say and shake hands. I try to pull away from Coal and put that wall up between us that I need. It's going to practically destroy me when he goes back to his life and I leave for Chicago.

"You and Kiera." Sheriff Kullen chuckles. "Take care of her and keep those punks at bay," he says, and I turn to look at him as Coal's body tightens behind me.

"Why are they such jerks?" Coal demands an answer.

Sheriff Kullen looks at me, and I beg him with my eyes not to say anything. I can't lose Coal yet.

"It's just young adults being stupid assholes," he says before he nods and pulls away from us.

"Hugh is the sheriff here?" Coal asks me.

"Yeah, he was voted in after his father died two years ago. He was hit by a drunk driver," I say.

"You and Hugh know each other?"

"Only through work. I used to work at Denny's as a server. He would come in."

"Okay," Coal says, and I feel the tension leave his body. He guides me up the stairs and into his mother's gallery. I look around having never been in here. The dust covered mural on the wall calls to me and I walk over to it, my fingers lightly tracing it. Something about it feels special and I step back into Coal's body.

"A friend of my mom's did that. I think it was your mother. That's why I brought you here," he whispers against my ear. I look down in the corner and find the artist's initials, MEJ. My body convulses and my knees buckle as I reach for it.

I cry out as the pain of seeing her work overtakes me.

"She was so talented. I took her away." I sob as Coal holds me against his body. He slides down to the dirty floor holding me in his arms as I cry for a mother I never knew.

"I've got you, pixie. Let it out." Coal's words break through my pain. "It's her, isn't it?" he asks, and I nod. "Want to see another picture?"

I tip my head back and look up into his beautiful face. He's given me something no one ever has. My mother.

"Yes."

He stands and lifts me up in his arms and

carries me over to a wall that leads to the back of the gallery. Pictures of artists that have presented their work here line the wall. My mother is in several of them alongside Coal's mother. She had dark hair just like me, and green eyes that shine through the old pictures. Her lips were full like mine. Her body curvier and fuller. There's a group shot with my father in the background. Anger etched on his face. I tremble and Coal holds me tighter.

"What is it? Is it too much? Do you want to leave?"

"He was angry even back then? They said he loved her and smiled only for her."

"Who, pixie?"

My answer would lead to so many more questions from him.

"Never mind." I shake my head. "Can we go now?"

"Yeah."

❖

Coal

. . .

I carry her out to my rental and buckle her into the passenger seat. I never expected her to react the way she did. It's as if she'd never seen her mother's work, and that doesn't make sense. Earlier she had told me she was going to art school in Chicago, that like her mother, she wanted to be an artist.

I climb back up the stairs and lock the gallery as I look around me. Darkness is settling in and I realize it's already after six in the evening. I need to feed her again, and I want to bury myself in her body for the rest of the night. I don't know where this is going, but I know I need to have her. That she is mine and meant to be with me.

I'm supposed to sign the reenlistment papers for another four years when I get back after the holiday, and that was my plan until I saw Kiera. Now I want to be with her. The thought of being away from her tears me apart. I swing up into the SUV and make my way over to Brick Oven Pizza, where I run in and order us a pepperoni, sausage, and mushroom with extra cheese to go.

My pixie likes pizza just the way I do. When we get back to the house, I park in the garage next to a smaller SUV. I know that's the car she mentioned before that my father tried to give her. She will be driving away in that and taking it with her to

Chicago. That way I know how to find her. Something settles in me at that thought.

We eat outside on the covered porch in the back. I light a fire in the outdoor fireplace and hold her against my body, taking in the quiet of the night as the snow falls. She cuddles into me, settling something deep inside me. A feeling of peace I haven't felt since before my mother died.

"What's out there?" I point to a gazebo a bit away from the house.

"That's where the hot tub is."

"A hot tub?"

"Yeah."

"Hmm, I'll have to get that going so I can fuck you in it next time." I kiss the top of her head.

"I'm going to need to go home. I need clothes, and I work Monday at the cabins and campgrounds."

Her words cause my heart to beat faster. I don't want to be away from her at all. I need her to stay with me because when I leave for Nevada, it will be some time before I get to be with her.

"Can you stay with me again tonight?" I lift her up on my lap so she is straddling me.

"One more night," she says. Tomorrow I'm going to talk her into staying with me longer, but for right now, I carry her into the house and make love to her again.

When she falls asleep, I decide to explore the house after making sure the outdoor fireplace is out. I head upstairs and go through all the rooms. I find my father's room across the house from the master suite. It faces the front of the house. It's plain without lots of decorations except for the pictures of me and my mother that line the dresser. Next to the bed is a framed picture from their wedding. I'm so confused.

I step out of the room and see a large circular room full of windows. It overlooks the driveway and the lake in the distance. I step into the room and see it's pretty much bare except for a small table and chair that face the window. That's when I see an envelope with my name on it. I sit down and open it. It's the letter from my father Lee had mentioned.

An hour later, Kiera's hands slide across my shoulders. Her body presses into my back.

"I'd find him in this room looking out over the lake all the time. Last year when you were deployed, he'd sit here for hours. I worried he'd fall asleep in the chair and fall from it." Her voice is quiet as she whispers against my neck.

"I was wrong about everything. I thought it was

his fault she died. I thought he had cheated on her to hurt her. They loved each other, but not like a married couple, it was more like best friends. They had both slept with other people. My mother just didn't do it as often because of me. I blamed him because it took the heat off me. If I hadn't been at a party that night, she would still be alive." I choke on the words.

Earl explained everything in his letter. How he wasn't sure how to be a father. How they had agreed to have other relationships and stay married for me and for the money. How he loved her and regretted hurting her. How much he regretted me leaving. The fact he followed my career and wanted me to settle down and be safe. How much he loved me and how this house was meant to be a place for me to raise my family. He told me the gallery was mine to do with whatever I wanted. He even explained how he had found Kiera and took care of her for her mother, knowing mine would have wanted that.

"He was one of the few people that was nice to me. I really have nothing in this town to stay for." Her words hurt to hear. I reach around me and direct her to straddle my lap. Her bare core under my T-shirt is on my boxer covered cock. I reach between us and slide my fingers through her folds, feeling the release from our earlier lovemaking leaking from her body. Before either of us says another word, I adjust us so my cock is out and I slide her down the length.

Her head falls back and my mouth lands on her neck. Kissing her.

"You'll always have me, Kiera. This is us. This is our place," I say as I move her over me slowly with the dark lake in the background. I make love to her right there in a room that was my father's favorite, and where I learned that I needed more in my life.

I've been ungloved all weekend with her, wanting to plant my baby inside her so she can't leave me. She'll have to come with me to Nevada until I'm done. She'll always be mine. Her eyes focus on me, the green darker as her lids droop in her desire.

"Coal." She sighs my name as she comes.

I stand and pull out, then bend her over the table and enter her from behind. I grip her hips tight, knowing I'm leaving fingerprints on her skin. I work into her over and over until the tingles along my spine are too much, then I plant myself deep as she screams my name and I growl hers.

CHAPTER 5
KIERA

I come awake to Coal sliding his hand across my skin and turn to see him watching me.

"I love watching you sleep, pixie."

"Why do you call me that?"

"With your green eyes and small frame, you remind me of a fairy or a pixie," he says before he leans in and kisses me.

I want to ask him if what he said early this morning was real. Am I his? Is this our place now? Does he really want me? But I don't because I know once he knows the truth, he'll run just like everyone else, or he'll call me a freak too. When his fingers brush over my scars, I sigh feeling that healing again.

"Come on. Let's go get some breakfast, then I'll run you to your place so you can pick up some more clothes. I'm not letting you go until after Christmas. Besides, we need a Christmas tree."

"I don't celebrate Christmas."

"Why not?"

I can't tell him the real reason. It'll expose more of my freakiness.

"I live in a town that celebrates it year round. What's the point?" I lie.

"Come on, pixie."

Coal insisted on driving me to the house. I figure Leon is still hungover from last night's bender when I don't see movement inside.

"Stay here, I'll be right back." I jump out of the SUV and run up the trail to the shed. I can't have Coal seeing where I really live. The lock isn't on the door and I can't remember if I locked it when I left. I open the door and find Leon standing inside. I step back as I take in the anger on his wrinkled face. He looks like the devil himself.

"Where have you been, you little bitch?" he yells.

"I've been with a friend." I look at my sleeping bag that's now destroyed. The knife still dangles from his hand, feathers laying at his feet. My clothes are all destroyed too. My backpack ripped apart. "Why?" I beg as tears roll down my face.

"Murderers don't deserve anything," he growls.

"Murderer? What are you talking about?"

Coal's voice comes from behind me. My head drops. Now he knows.

"Didn't she tell you? She killed her mother."

"What?" Coal's voice sounds tortured, and I turn to defend myself.

"I didn't do it. I was a baby," I say, but he steps back from me. My heart breaks.

"Did she let you fuck her? Did you pay her good? Because she's going to need the bail money. I called the cops as soon as you pulled up for trespassing. I kicked her off my property a week ago," Leon yells.

"Shut up." I look at him. "I didn't kill her." I turn back to Coal. "Please, I didn't know how to tell you." I reach for him, and he takes my hand and pulls me out of the shed.

"Do you live in there? Is he telling the truth? Who is that?" His questions roll off his lips so fast.

"He's my father. I swear I didn't do it. I was a baby. Please don't leave me," I beg him.

"Murderer." My hair is pulled from behind me as Leon bellows. He swings me around and wraps his hand around my throat, squeezing hard. "You killed the only woman I ever loved. I've waited eighteen years for revenge."

I look up as his other hand comes down with

the knife aimed at my chest. I close my eyes knowing there is no way I'm going to come through this unscathed.

"No," Coal yells, and my eyes flare open in time to see him knock the knife away. Leon's nails rip into my throat as Coal pushes me away. I fall and land hard on the ground.

"Coal, no." I try to yell when I look over and see him punching Leon, but nothing comes out. Then the sirens break through everything.

"Let him go, Coal, now," the sheriff yells.

"He beat me up for no reason. Do your job and arrest them both." Leon's speech is slurred, his face bloody. My vision blurs but I force myself to keep watching.

"Call an ambulance," the sheriff says to someone.

"Pixie, are you okay?" Coal falls at my feet.

I try to answer him but the words are trapped in my throat. Then there is nothing.

A beeping sound, voices I don't recognize in the distance, and a smell I know all cross my senses as I open my eyes to a dim hospital room. I slip from the bed glad I'm not hooked up to an IV drip, and make my way across the room. I stand at the door and listen for a moment trying to see if Coal is out there.

"I'm sorry, Lee, but Leon has pressed charges." I hear the sheriff's voice. "The judge will see him tomorrow and decide on how to proceed."

I need to see Coal but I'm afraid he's going to blame me for the trouble he's in. I look around the room trying to find a way to escape without Sheriff Kullen and Mr. Rumble knowing. The only other door in the room leads to the bathroom. I look inside and am happy to find it's a Jack and Jill style with an attached room on the other side. After carefully checking to make sure the other room is empty, I return to my room and slip the pillows under the blanket, making it look like I'm in the bed sleeping. I look down at my clothes, they are dirty but still mine. I find my shoes near the bed and slip them on. I'm quiet as I sneak into the next room. Peeking out the door, I see the nurses at the desk but no one else. It looks the sheriff and Mr. Rumble have dispersed. I exit the room and move down the hall, careful not to draw attention to myself. When I make it to the hospital entrance, I keep walking until I reach the curb and hail a taxi. I give the driver my address. It's the only place I can think of to hide where no one would look for me, and I'm hoping some of my clothes survived Leon's anger.

After spending the night in the shed, where I used my jacket and paint canvases to keep myself warm, I'm now standing in line at the bank waiting for my turn. Leon thankfully didn't come home, and the sheriff didn't find me. I'm in the only pair of jeans that didn't get cut up. These plus the pair I had from Coal's house are all the jeans I have to my name. I found out the judge granted Coal bail. I can't afford the full bail, but I can pay his bond, which is five thousand dollars. I've already paid for the first semester of art school, and what's left in my bank account was to help with finding an apartment and my travel. It's everything I have, but Coal doesn't need to suffer for my problems.

Taking a deep breath, I walk into the sheriff's station and right up to the counter after taking care of Coal's bond. He wouldn't be in here if it weren't for me. If he had never met me, he'd be safe in his big house away from me and my fucked-up past.

"I want to see Sheriff Kullen," I say to the woman behind the counter.

"Pixie?" I turn to see Coal being led by sheriff's deputies into the lobby.

"I'm so sorry. It's all my fault." I rush to him, but a deputy steps in front of me and stops me.

"I'm sorry, miss, you can't come any closer."

"Are you okay?" Coal asks, looking around the deputy. "God, I thought he was going to kill you. I couldn't lose you, Kiera. I love you."

"I..." He loves me?

"Staff Sergeant Bridger, you need to come with us." I turn to see men in military uniforms with guns on their hips and a pair of shackles in their hands.

"No. You can't take him. I paid the bond. He should be able to leave."

"I'm sorry, ma'am, he must come with us."

"No." I step between them and Coal. "He didn't do it. He was protecting me. Please," I beg.

"Kiera, they need to take him. With the holidays and court not being in session for a few days, the judge decided the military could have jurisdiction. He has to go with them." Sheriff Kullen pulls me out of between everyone.

"He was saving me. Please, don't take him. He's the only person that's ever loved me." I plea with everything in me.

"Be strong, pixie. You can do this. I love you."

"No, Coal, I need you." I crumple as I watch them cuff him.

"I love you," he says again.

"Don't go, I have no one else. Nothing left." I pull away from the sheriff. "I love you too." One of the guards pushes me back.

"Get your hands off her. She's carrying my baby," Coal yells at them and fights against the cuffs.

Sheriff Kullen grabs me again and holds me back tighter. "I got her, Coal," he says, and I watch and scream until I lose my voice as they take him away from me. I cry so hard I black out.

Coal

"Happy fucking birthday to me. Merry fucking Christmas," I say to the quiet of the room. I've been on lockdown in a barrack room since they brought me back to base yesterday. I haven't seen Kiera in two days, but I've dreamt of her every night. I've had nightmares as I watched that knife plunging toward her chest.

I don't know if she's pregnant with my child or not, but I told the SFs she was to keep them from hurting her. I can still hear her voice as she screamed for me. She said I was the only person to love her. I think of the weekend I spent making love to her. Every time we did, I was telling her without words how I felt about her. It's a torture I'll hold onto until they figure out what my punishment is.

A knock sounds on my door.

"Enter."

The door opens and Lee steps inside.

"I hope you know I'm charging you not only for travel expenses but double time for working on the holiday."

"Whatever. None of it matters."

"The sheriff dropped the charges after Kiera told them the whole story. They found the knife on Leon at the hospital. So stop the pity party and take whatever punishment the military has in store for you. You're a free man, according to the civilian government."

"Thank God."

"But you're still charged with conduct unbecoming for continuing to hit Leon after you disarmed him."

"He was going to kill her." I rip my hands through my hair. "How is she?"

"I don't know." His words cut through me.

"What do you mean?"

"She's been missing ever since she broke out of the hospital again yesterday."

"You need to find her, Lee."

"I'll try, but I'm trying to help you here."

"I don't care, they can take away everything from me, but I can't lose her. Is she in Chicago? Go there." That's where she was planning to move.

"She blamed herself for you being taken into custody. She cleared out her bank account to pay the bond before I could intervene, and the bail bondsman won't refund the money even though charges have been dropped." Something passes across his eyes before he looks down. And again, his words are like a knife to my soul.

"Find her. Give her everything. She'll have a place to stay at least, until I can get back to her if she ever forgives me. Find her and take care of her. I'll take whatever punishment they determine for me here." I look up at him and see the sorrow in his eyes.

"Coal, the will is still in probate. I can't give her

the house. The only thing in your name is the gallery."

"How is that in my name and not the house?"

"Your father put it in your name right after you left."

"Give it to her."

"But it's all you have from your mother."

"I don't care. She needs to be safe. She gave everything for me, I'll do the same for her."

"Coal, they arrested Leon. She'll be safe." He tries to assure me.

I shake my head. "She'll never be safe in that town as long as they believe what Leon said. What really happened to her mother?"

"I'll find out." He assures me and leaves me alone.

I spend the rest of Christmas in my room, waiting until they decide what they are going to do to me.

CHAPTER 6
KIERA

It's been more than a week since I last saw Coal, since they took him away from me. Lee found me a couple days after Christmas hiding in the old cabin Earl had lived in. I skipped work and cried for days, eating very little. By the time he found me, I was dehydrated. and again ended up in the hospital. He told the doctors there was a high likelihood I was pregnant, but they said it was too early to tell. They treated me as such anyway, just in case. I was given fluids and spent the night in the hospital. The next day Lee showed up and told me I could stay at Coal's mom's gallery.

"There is a small apartment upstairs you can stay in," Lee says as we pull up in front of the gallery. "It's yours to do with as you please. Coal wanted you to have it." His words hurt because that means Coal isn't coming back. For the first Christmas ever, I actually felt loved, until this moment. I nod at him and take the keys before stepping out of the car.

Now I'm sitting here watching as the town celebrates the new year around me. Fireworks will go off over the lake at midnight. I need to make it to the store to buy eggs and milk. I slip on my tennis shoes and my coat. It's cooler today and the snow is sticking. I step out of the gallery's back door and lock it behind me. I'm careful across the parking lot, I don't want to slip and fall. I still don't know if I'm pregnant, but if I am, I'm going to give this baby everything I didn't have.

Stepping into the warm interior of the grocery store, I grab a cart and walk down the aisles. I found out I still have my job cleaning the cabins and I start again the day after tomorrow. All my bruises from Leon's attack have faded to yellow. Leon is in jail, and Sheriff Kullen said he won't get out for a long time. I'm sad to say I'm actually hurt I caused all this strife.

"Freak. Murderer," is hissed from behind me, and I turn to see Barbie, my old manager from the country club, standing at the end of the aisle. "You ruined that poor man's life with your filth."

"No, I didn't." I cry.

"Yes, you did."

"My life isn't ruined." Coal's voice comes from

behind me, and I twist so fast I lose my footing. He rushes to me and catches me. "Pixie, be careful."

"Coal." I cry.

"Just a second." He pulls me into him, and I hold on with everything in me as he looks over my head to Barbie. "You're fired. I run that country club now, and I don't want people that bully others working for me. Besides, Kiera didn't kill anyone. Leon killed his own wife when he didn't take her to the hospital when she started hemorrhaging. Kiera was only a newborn at the time."

His words seep into my soul and heal something deep inside me.

"No one bullies my fiancée and gets away with it. She's now a Bridger, and you'll show her the respect she is due as my wife," he says as he swings me up into his arms.

I cry into his neck until I feel him settle me into the passenger seat of a large vehicle. I look up and see it's a Jeep.

"Where are we going?" I ask as he buckles me in.

"Home, pixie."

I smile at him as I watch him walk around the Jeep and climb up into the driver's side.

"What happened?"

"I was given the choice to not reenlist and still keep my rank. I took the offer and drove home. I have a woman to take care of. A baby hopefully on the way. A gallery to open, and a town to scare." He smiles at me and that dimple pops out.

"I love you," I say to him.

"Don't say that until I have my cock in you, pixie," he growls, and I laugh at him.

We pull up to the house and he opens the garage and pulls in next to the SUV his father bought me.

"Next time you leave the house, you'll take that car." He points at me and all I can do is nod at him. I wouldn't have a driver's license if Earl hadn't taken me to get it.

"Is it true what you said about my mother?"

"Yeah, Lee requested the coroner's report and then questioned Leon. You didn't kill her. It was a tragic event. He didn't take her to the hospital because he didn't want others around her. He was jealous of everyone, even you."

I open my door and go to step out. "Stay there, pixie, keep your ass in that seat." I do as he says, and he comes around to lift me out of the Jeep. He steps into the house and sets me down. We take off our coats and shoes in the utility room before entering the main house. He pulls me along behind him to the dining room. Standing there is Lee and a man I don't recognize, along with Sheriff Kullen.

"What's going on?" I ask him, and when I turn around, he is down on his knee.

"Pixie, I'd go to jail for you. I'd give up everything for you. From the moment I saw you, I knew you were meant to be mine. I want to show you that Christmas is special, and that you are special. I want to see you in every room of this house. Your art, your presence, your smell. I want to heal all the pain your father caused you. I want to show you what love really is. And, even if you aren't carrying my baby right now, you will be soon. I want babies with you, lots of them. Please make me the happiest man and marry me. I know it's soon, but I know you are meant to be mine."

My hand flies to my mouth. He knows everything about me and yet he still wants me. "I love you, Coal. Yes to all of it. I want you too." I lean down and kiss him on the lips. He stands and pulls me into his arms.

"I love you, Kiera." His mouth descends down to mine, kissing me, his tongue sliding between my lips as his arms wrap around me.

"Okay, can we get this show on the road? It's a

busy night for me." Sheriff Kullen interrupts. We part and turn back to the group.

I walk through the house and stop at the window overlooking the lake. Small groups of fireworks go off as people get ready to celebrate to the new year. Coal is showing everyone out the door. I just married him in jeans and a hoodie, but I didn't care about a dress. All I cared about was becoming his wife and having him forever. Sheriff Kullen signed as my witness and Lee signed for Coal. I am now Mrs. Coal Bridger.

I spin around with my arms flying out. The feeling of not only freedom but peace overwhelms me.

"That's the most beautiful thing I've ever seen." Coal's voice comes from the entrance to the living room. I stop my spinning and face him.

"I can't believe this is happening."

"It is, pixie. I wanted to start the new year as your husband. A new us. I'm going to show you every day for the rest of your life that you are special and loved."

I walk toward him and reach up when I'm right up against him.

"Coal, you're the special one for giving me this life."

He leans down and kisses me but doesn't stop there. He lifts me into his arms and carries me upstairs where he makes love to me over and over. At midnight, he kisses me. He's made my holidays perfect, and I know he'll keep doing that for years to come.

EPILOGUE
KIERA

"Hello, my little Ava girl." Coal's voice comes from the baby monitor and I smile. "Is Momma in her studio?" I look over at the monitor screen and see my husband reach into the crib to lift up our daughter. He makes his way to the rocking chair where he sits with her. "Did Daddy ever tell you about his name? Your grandma named me Coal because I was so small and born on Christmas Day. She said that if you squeezed a lump of coal hard enough, it would become a diamond. Of course, that isn't true, but she always joked about it." I smile at his story.

Coal got me pregnant the first night we ever made love, and in September, our baby girl was born. He was worried the whole pregnancy, even when the doctor confirmed over and over that I was healthy and there was nothing to worry about. After Ava was born, he kept an even closer eye on me, worried that I would hemorrhage just like my mom had, but I didn't.

I look out the windows across the lake and back to my painting. The gallery has been open for only a few months, but it's been an even bigger hit than before. Not only do local artists show their work, but I've got a long list of well-known artists wanting to show there too. My work is always on display, even though Coal tries to buy it all and keep it for himself.

My father was sentenced and we haven't heard anything from him since. After he went to jail, we bought the house when it was foreclosed on. Not for sentimental reasons, but to take possession of my mother's things. Now all of her artwork is on display in the gallery and our home. Sheriff Kullen is a regular guest and friend of ours. He often differs to Coal on emergency management suggestions and has talked him into running for a community seat. Coal runs his father's business, and now the town doesn't call his dad Mr. Bah Humbug anymore. Some residents still can be mean to me, but they never do it in front of Coal.

"Hello, pixie." Coal's voice breaks me from my thoughts. I quickly wipe my hands off on my smock and then slip it off. "Wow, this is beautiful," he says as he takes in the painting I'm working on.

"Thank you. How was your meeting?"

"It was interrupted, Hugh had to take off on a call."

"Oh, I hope everyone is safe." Sheriff Kullen is up for reelection next year and is trying to be on top of everything. I worry our friend is pushing himself too much.

"It wasn't that kind of call." He smirks at me.

"Really? Do you think he has a girlfriend?"

"Pixie, no gossip. He'll tell us when he's ready. Now, are you and Ava ready for her first time on Santa's lap?"

"I have the perfect outfit picked out for her."

This year Coal is trying to erase all my Christmases past. Every day is a new experience.

He pulls me into his arms and holds me tightly before leaning down to kiss me.

"You're my diamond." I sigh when he releases my lips. "Your mom was right. I held on tight to you."

"I'd sacrifice it all again for you, my love."

"Me too."

I'll never regret not going to art school because everything I've ever wanted is right here.

Love, family, and home.

CHRISTMAS OF LOVE
COLLABORATION

Other books releasing in the Christmas of Love collection are as follows and can be read as complete standalone stories in any order.

13 Nights of Christmas by Emily Rose
Coal For Kiera by E.M. Shue
Fabricated Christmas by Glenna Maynard
Finding Mistletoe by AJ Alexander
Finding Mrs. Claus by Leaona Luxx
Holiday Wishes by S.L. Sterling
Holly's Knight by KL Donn
Merry & Bright by Mayra Statham
Secretly Sant by B.L. Olson
The Christmas Proposition by Mika Jolie
Wedding Bell Rock by Annelise Reynolds & Dawn Sullivan

Find all information about each book on the
Alluring Write Productions website.

COMING SOON

Her Empire: Mafia Made Series

From award winning author E.M. Shue comes a new dark mafia romance written in USA Today Bestselling Author KL Donn's Mafia Made World.

Anatonia is a killer. Until Vitaly comes for her. Now she will protect the hitman.

Anatonia is the head bodyguard for the Morello Mafia. She will kill anyone that comes close to Posy for Natale Morello. It's what she was raised to do.

Kill.

She's one of the deadliest hitmen to come out of MI6, KGB and even survived special forces Marine training at a young age. But few know she is the niece to the head of the deadly Bocharov

Russian family. That he raised her to destroy the Morello's.

Because she defied him, he's sent his best killer to kill her.

Vitaly is the monster in the dark.

He's the one the Bocharov family sends to end their enemies. He thinks he's only been sent to kill a rival family's enforcer. What he doesn't know is she is the illegitimate niece to his boss and now the woman he will do anything for.

Even defy the family he's bled for. He'll protect her and help her conquer her enemies.

The Bocharov Family has declared war against Anatonia, and she will end them.

Can Vitaly hold the woman he was born to protect? Will Anatonia still be standing when the blood of an Empire is destroyed?

Will they kill the Empire she was meant to lead?

Add to your TBR: http:// bit.ly/HerEmpireGoodreads

Coal for Keira: Christmas of Love Collaboration

Confined Space: KB Everyday Heroes World (Coming 2021)

Her Empire: Mafia Made World (Coming 2021)

Eternal: Salvation Society (Coming 2021)

Until Tucker: HEA (Coming 2021)

ACKNOWLEDGMENTS

Happy Holidays everyone!

The Holidays are always hard for some people and I completely understand that, because I've had my own struggles with them. Like I said in the dedication this book is for you. No matter what your beliefs are someone is always willing to listen.

All the other authors in this collaboration, thank you for all the sharing and support. KL thank you for putting this together and forcing me to jump out of my own worlds and try something new. You're the best!

My Hubby: Love you babe, here's another one for you.

My Girls: Paige, you're the best with all your help and support. I love you being my PA.

Kelsey, I love you and wish you knew how much.

Daniele, thank you for letting me write about a condition you struggle with. I'm proud of you and always know I'm here to listen when the urge gets too much.

My Silent Partner: You're the best. Love you lady!!

My Family: Mom, grandma, my brothers, sisters, sisters-in-law, brothers-in-law, my aunts, my uncles, cousins, nieces, nephews, adopted family, foster family, doggies, and grand doggies, you all help and support in your own way and I appreciate all of you. Happy Holidays to you all!

My Editor: Thank you for sticking with me and supporting me.

My ARC & Street Team: Thank you all so much.

My Surprises: You all are so awesome and supportive.

My support team: The authors, bloggers, Pas, and readers that support me I appreciate all your hard work in sharing, advise and help. Thank you!

Finally: You the reader, you're the best. Thank you for reading my words, without you I would have quit a long time ago. Hope you all loved Coal and Kiera as much as I do.

BIO

Writer, wife, mother of three girls, doggie mom to one, and doggie grandma to four. This multi-published award-winning author likes her whiskey Irish, her chocolate dark and her hockey hard hitting. She's an avid reader and you can find her Kindle packed full of all sub-genres of romance. When she isn't writing action-adventure, suspense, and strong woman she's spending time with her family exploring Alaska.

She's currently writing the hot and steamy romantic suspense series Securities International, the novella insta-love series The Caine & Graco Saga, the dark MC/Mafia Knights of Purgatory Syndicate series, several standalones in multiple worlds, and soon to come the insta-love action-adventure CGS New York Rescue series, a spin-off of the Caine & Graco Saga.

Three of her books have won the Colorado

RWA Beverley contest, Sniper's Kiss in 2018 for Suspense, Angel's Kiss in 2019 for Contemporary, and Accidentally Noah in 2020 for Suspense, while many others were finalists in this same contest.

E.M.'s favorite saying is don't piss her off she'll write you into a book and kill you off in a new and gory way.

Join Cocktails & Friends to be kept up to date on all her new releases and appearances. [https:// bit.ly/EMDrinkswithfriends]

Follow her on these platforms:

Website: https://bit.ly/authoremshue

Twitter: https://bit.ly/EMShueTwitter

Facebook: https://bit.ly/EMShueFB

E.M. Surprises - fun, games, excerpts and more: https://bit.ly/EMSurprises

Amazon: https://bit.ly/EMShueAmazon

Instagram: https://bit.ly/EMShueInstagram

Bookbub: https://bit.ly/EMShue_BB

Goodreads: https://bit.ly/EMShueGR

Made in the USA
Coppell, TX
19 November 2020

41625824R10066